Bee Gets a Sweater

Written by Keith Faulkner

Illustrated by Jonathan Lambert

Long, long ago when all bees were just plain black, Bee was buzzing around the flowers, collecting the nectar to make honey.

"Brr! I'm freezing," said Bee to Spider, who was hanging from a thread nearby.

"If you'd like, I'll knit a warm sweater for you," replied Spider, who was very good at knitting.

Having so many legs, Spider was a very quick knitter. By the very next day she was finished.

Spider didn't mind at all. She had lots of different colored yarns and enjoyed having something to do. "What about this one?" she asked.

"What do you think?" she said to Bee, as he tried on the green and purple striped sweater.

"Um... Sorry, but I don't think it suits me," replied Bee.
How the other animals laughed at the sight!

"Mmm! A bit bright!" said Bee, looking down and blinking at the bright orange sweater with pink zigzags.

Spider's knitting needles started clicking away again, and soon the next sweater was finished.

"Oh! Bright blue and red squares," gasped Bee. "Very colorful, but it's not really my style."

"Don't worry, I've got lots of ideas," laughed Spider, reaching for her needles.

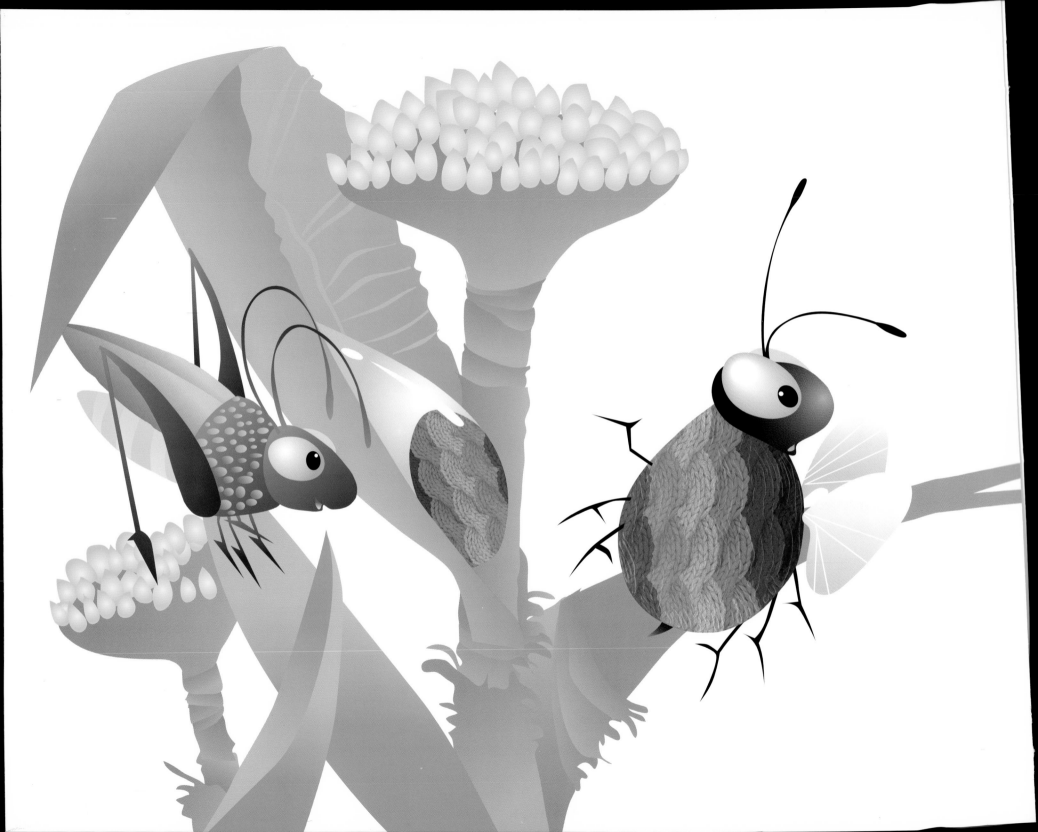

"Now, that is different," said Bee, carrying on Spider's latest creation. "I love rainbows!"

"I used every color in my knitting bag," said Spider proudly.

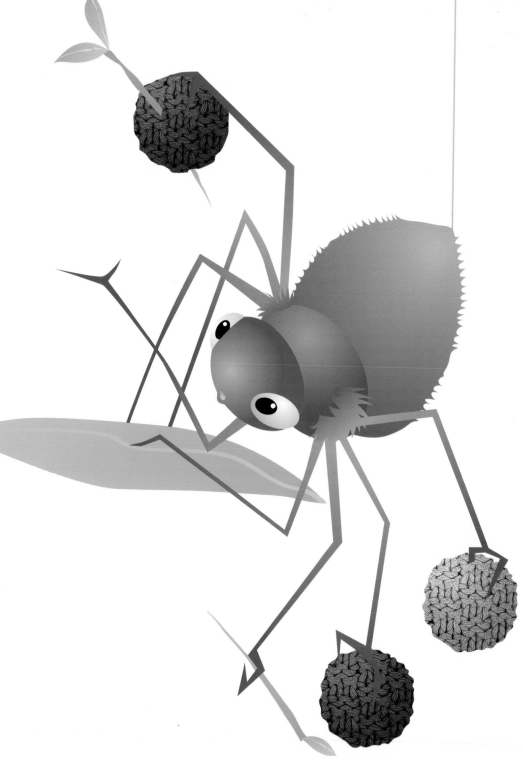

"But there's just too many colors," sighed Bee.

"Close your eyes," said Spider, "and try this one on."
Bee closed his eyes and slipped
on the new sweater.